D1266721

# Two Scarlet Songbirds

*A Story of Anton Dvořák*

by Carole Lexa Schaefer
illustrated by Elizabeth Rosen

Alfred A. Knopf New York

To my Czech-American family and the music they put in my ears
—C.L.S.

For Mark, Cody, and Little Bean, with all my love
—E.R.

THIS IS A BORZOI BOOK PUBLISHED BY ALFRED A. KNOPF



Hand-lettering by David Coulson.

www.randomhouse.com/kids

*Library of Congress Cataloging-in-Publication Data*
Schaefer, Carole Lexa.
Two scarlet songbirds / by Carole Lexa Schaefer ; illustrated by Elizabeth Rosen. — 1st ed.
p. cm.
Summary: While visiting Iowa in 1893, the Czech composer Anton Dvořák hears the song of a scarlet tanager and is inspired to create a new piece of music.
ISBN 0-375-81022-6 (trade)—ISBN 0-375-91022-0 (lib. bdg.)
1. Dvořák, Antonín, 1841–1904—Juvenile Fiction. [1. Dvořák, Antonín, 1841–1904—Fiction. 2. Composers—Fiction. 3. Music—Fiction. 4. Scarlet tanager—Fiction. 5. Birds—Fiction.] I. Rosen, Elizabeth, 1961– ill. II. Title.
PZ7.S3315 Tw 2001
[Fic]—dc21 00-061514

Printed in the United States of America
September 2001

10 9 8 7 6 5 4 3 2 1 First Edition

On a June day in 1893, a man and a bird traveled toward the same place in the state of Iowa on the Turkey River.

The red bird flew on black wings high above a dirt road. It was searching for somewhere to settle in the woods near the river.

Below the flying bird, the man—with whiskers on his chin and music in his head—rolled along the road in an open buggy. He was making his first visit to the river town of Spillville, where he and his family planned to spend the summer.

The bird was Scarlet Tanager—a singer of songs. The man was Anton Dvořák—a famous composer of music.

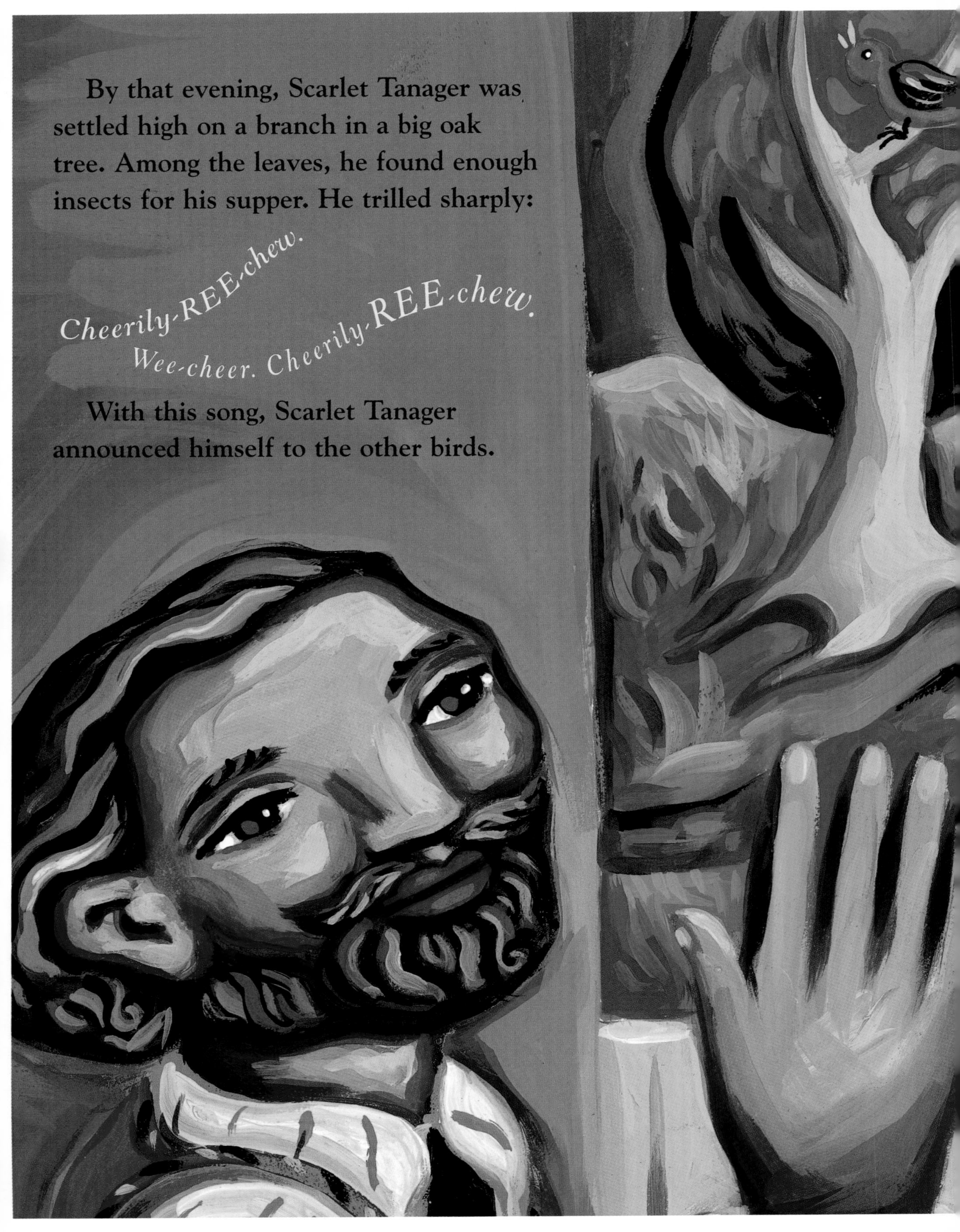

By that evening, Scarlet Tanager was settled high on a branch in a big oak tree. Among the leaves, he found enough insects for his supper. He trilled sharply:

*Cheerily-REE-chew. Cheerily-REE-chew.*
*Wee-cheer. Cheerily-REE-chew.*

With this song, Scarlet Tanager announced himself to the other birds.

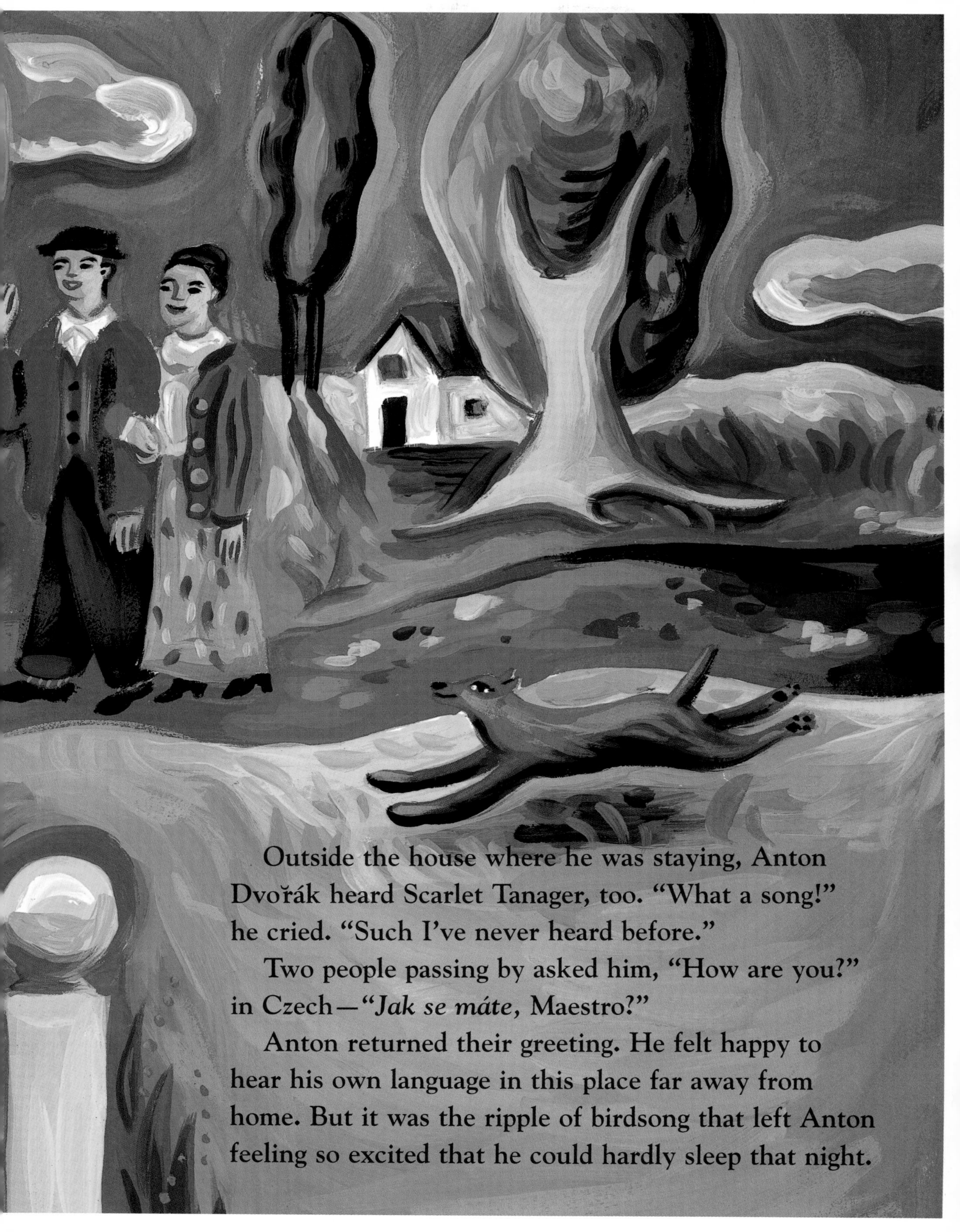

Outside the house where he was staying, Anton Dvořák heard Scarlet Tanager, too. "What a song!" he cried. "Such I've never heard before."

Two people passing by asked him, "How are you?" in Czech—"*Jak se máte,* Maestro?"

Anton returned their greeting. He felt happy to hear his own language in this place far away from home. But it was the ripple of birdsong that left Anton feeling so excited that he could hardly sleep that night.

Before dawn the next day, Scarlet Tanager was up. He fluttered, and ate, and soared—all the while singing and calling:

*Cheer-REE. Cheerily-ree . . .*

*Cheerily-WHEE-chew . . .*
*Ree-cheer-cheer.*

The songs of many birds filled the morning air.

But as dawn grew rosy, Scarlet Tanager preened and sang for just one yellow-breasted female tanager. She chose to stay close beside him.

Dawn was not too early for Maestro Anton Dvořák. He sat on a stump near the big oak, surrounded by the birds in their morning concert.

He whispered, "Now to watch and listen. And hopefully," he added, "to find that wonderful creature I heard singing last night."

Scarlet Tanager and his mate quietly filled the afternoon with work.

*Twish*, pick, pluck.

They gathered up grass, twigs, and fluff.

High up on a branch in the oak, they began to pack and weave, weave and pack their bits of stuff together into a new nest.

During the quiet afternoon, Anton Dvořák, carrying his violin, strolled along the river.

He saw bright water rushing along under the footbridge.

*Lap-a-tuh-lup.*

He smelled sweet flowering grasses.

Ahh.

He heard a woman sharply call her geese.

Husa, husa!

A breeze fluttered, cool against Anton's summer hot face.

Shoosh.

He remembered morning birdsong.

*Cheerily-REE-cheer.*

Maestro Anton worked, trying to weave these bits together into a new piece of music.

**Think**, pick, pluck.

All that long June evening, Scarlet Tanager and his mate sat near their nest singing:

*Cheer-REE. Cheerily-ree.*

*Cheerily-whee. Cheer-REE-chew.*

Anton spent the evening in his snug workroom. He sat with Frank, a Spillville boy who liked birds as much as Anton did. They matched bird sounds from Anton's notes with Frank's bird sketches and names.

Wick-wick-wick-wick-wick.

"That's a flicker laughing, Maestro," joked Frank.

Kuka-kuka-kuka.

"The first time I heard that one, I thought it was a frog," said Frank. "But my granny said, 'No, it's a black-billed cuckoo.'"

"There's one bird's song I've tried to capture," said Anton. "But it's hard to write down and hard to play." He plinked on the keys of his borrowed piano. "It sounds something like—

*Cheerily, cheer, cheer-REE-chew.*"

"Ahh, Granny calls that one Robin-with-a-Sore-Throat," said Frank. "But it's really Scarlet Tanager. Keep looking for him. Up high. He's worth it."

On the third morning, in his tree by the river, Scarlet Tanager trilled out nesting songs, mating songs, and warning songs for all to hear.

On the ground below, Maestro Anton Dvořák lay on his back looking up. He tried to catch glimpses of the scarlet songbird darting about high in the canopy of oak leaves.

The bird's songs drifted down to Anton:

*Whee-cheer.*
*Cheerily-REE-chew.*

Anton sat up. In his notebook, he wrote and wrote a mix of bird sounds and his own music notes.

When the notebook was full, Anton wrote on the stiff white cuffs of his long-sleeved shirt. When those were full, he headed home.

Some days later, Scarlet Tanager was flying near the house of the schoolmaster.

Inside, by an open window, Anton Dvořák stood playing the violin.

Three other musicians played, too, on a violin, a viola, and a cello. Their music was the "American Quartet"—a new work by Anton Dvořák.

As Scarlet Tanager flew by, Anton bowed the strings of his violin. The opening notes of the third movement of his music drifted out.

*Cheer-REE. Cheerily-ree.*

In mid-flight, Scarlet Tanager stopped. He perched on a branch to listen to the song that, in a new voice, sounded so much like his own.

Anton's song went on.
Scarlet Tanager opened his beak.
For the period of one long trill—

*Cheer-REE. Cheerily-ree. Cheerily-whee. Cheer-REE-chew*

two scarlet songbirds
sang together.

Then, while one played on,
the other . . .

. . . flew home.

# Author's Note

In the fall of 1892, the famous Czech composer Antonín (or Anton, as he is often known in America) Dvořák left his home in the city of Prague to live in New York City and serve as the director of the National Conservatory of Music. His work was to teach American musicians and composers, and to write music and direct concerts. He brought his wife and two of his six children along with him.

Anton liked much about being in New York City, but by springtime he was homesick for his other children and for his summer home near Prague. He planned to go back there for his four months of summer vacation. Instead, Anton's assistant, Josef Kovařík, convinced him to bring the rest of his family to the United States and to take them all for the summer to Josef's hometown of Spillville, Iowa, on the Turkey River.

Spillville was a farm town settled by people who had come to America from Czechoslovakia. Josef knew that Anton would be interested in meeting these people. He also knew that Spillville was a place rich in the sights and sounds of water, gentle winds, and, especially, birdsong—things in nature to which Anton Dvořák often responded by making new music.

And Josef Kovařík was right. In the first few days after arriving in Spillville, Maestro Dvořák composed the American Quartet, a string quartet in F major. The third movement of this music was inspired by the song of the Scarlet Tanager—a bird that Anton Dvořák had never seen or heard before.

In *Two Scarlet Songbirds*, historical fact and imagination are woven together to create a telling of how this lovely piece of music came to be.